Amelia Bedelia

Amelia Bedelia

by Peggy Parish

pictures by Fritz Siebel

HarperCollins*Publishers*

Amelia Bedelia Text copyright © 1963 by Margaret Parish Text copyright renewed 1991 by the Estate of Margaret Parish Illustrations copyright © 1963 by Fritz Siebel Illustrations copyright renewed 1991 by Fritz Siebel Revised illustrations copyright © 1992 by the Estate of Fritz Siebel All rights reserved. No part of this book may be used or reproduced in any manner whatsoever without written permission except in the case of brief quotations embodied in critical articles and reviews. Manufactured in China. For information address HarperCollins Children's Books, a division of HarperCollins Publishers, 195 Broadway, New York, NY 10007. www.harperchildrens.com

Library of Congress Cataloging-in-Publication Data
Parish, Peggy.
    Amelia Bedelia / by Peggy Parish ; pictures by Fritz Siebel. — New ed.
       p.   cm. — (An I can read book)
    Summary: A literal-minded housekeeper causes a ruckus in the household when she attempts to make sense of some instructions.
    ISBN 978-0-06-020186-9 (trade bdg.)
    ISBN 978-0-06-020187-6 (lib. bdg.)
    ISBN 978-0-06-444155-1 (pbk.)
    [1. Humorous stories.] I. Siebel, Fritz, ill. II. Title. III. Series.
PZ7.P219Am 1992   91-10163
[E]—dc20   CIP
                                                                                                                     AC

14 15 16 17 18 SCP 20 19 18
❖

For Debbie, John Grier,
Walter, and Michael Dinkins

"Oh, Amelia Bedelia,

your first day of work,

and I can't be here.

But I made a list for you.

You do just what the list says,"

said Mrs. Rogers.

Mrs. Rogers got into the car

with Mr. Rogers.

They drove away.

"My, what nice folks.

I'm going to like working here,"

said Amelia Bedelia.

Amelia Bedelia went inside.

"Such a grand house.

These must be rich folks.

But I must get to work.

Here I stand just looking.

And me with a whole list

of things to do."

Amelia Bedelia stood there

a minute longer.

"I think I'll make

a surprise for them.

I'll make lemon-meringue pie.

I do make good pies."

So Amelia Bedelia went
into the kitchen.
She put a little of this
and a pinch of that
into a bowl.
She mixed and she rolled.

Soon her pie was ready

to go into the oven.

"There," said Amelia Bedelia.

"That's done."

"Now let's see what this list says."

Amelia Bedelia read,

Change the towels in the green bathroom.

Amelia Bedelia found

the green bathroom.

"Those towels are very nice.

Why change them?" she thought.

Then Amelia Bedelia remembered

what Mrs. Rogers had said.

She must do just what

the list told her.

"Well, all right,"

said Amelia Bedelia.

Amelia Bedelia got some scissors.

She snipped a little here

and a little there.

And she changed those towels.

"There," said Amelia Bedelia.

She looked at her list again.

Dust the furniture.

"Did you ever hear tell

of such a silly thing.

At my house we undust the furniture.

But to each his own way."

Amelia Bedelia took

one last look at the bathroom.

She saw a big box with the words

Dusting Powder on it.

"Well, look at that.

A special powder to dust with!"

exclaimed Amelia Bedelia.

So Amelia Bedelia

dusted the furniture.

"That should be dusty enough.

My, how nice it smells."

Draw the drapes when the sun comes in.

read Amelia Bedelia.

She looked up.

The sun was coming in.

Amelia Bedelia looked

at the list again.

"Draw the drapes?

That's what it says.

I'm not much

of a hand at drawing,

but I'll try."

So Amelia Bedelia sat right down
and she drew those drapes.

Amelia Bedelia
marked off
about the drapes.
"Now what?"

Put the lights out when you finish in the living room.

Amelia Bedelia

thought about this a minute.

She switched off the lights.

Then she carefully

unscrewed each bulb.

And Amelia Bedelia
put the lights out.
"So those things need
to be aired out, too.
Just like pillows and babies.
Oh, I do have a lot to learn."

"My pie!" exclaimed Amelia Bedelia.
She hurried to the kitchen.

"Just right," she said.

She took the pie out of the oven

and put it on the table to cool.

Then she looked at the list.

Measure two cups of rice.

"That's next," said Amelia Bedelia.

Amelia Bedelia found two cups.

She filled them with rice.

34

And Amelia Bedelia

measured that rice.

Amelia Bedelia laughed.

"These folks

do want me to do funny things."

Then she poured the rice

back into the container.

The meat market will deliver a steak and a chicken.

Please trim the fat before you put the steak in the icebox.

And please dress the chicken.

When the meat arrived,

Amelia Bedelia opened the bag.

She looked at the steak

for a long time.

"Yes," she said.

"That will do nicely."

Amelia Bedelia got some lace

and bits of ribbon.

And Amelia Bedelia

trimmed that fat

before she put

the steak in the icebox.

"Now I must dress the chicken.

I wonder if she wants

a he chicken or a she chicken?"

said Amelia Bedelia.

Amelia Bedelia went right to work.

Soon the chicken was finished.

Amelia Bedelia heard the door open.

"The folks are back," she said.

She rushed out to meet them.

"Amelia Bedelia,

why are all the light bulbs outside?"

asked Mr. Rogers.

"The list just said

to put the lights out,"

said Amelia Bedelia.

"It didn't say to bring them back in.

Oh, I do hope

they didn't get aired too long."

47

"Amelia Bedelia,

the sun will fade the furniture.

I asked you to draw the drapes,"

said Mrs. Rogers.

"I did! I did! See,"

said Amelia Bedelia.

She held up her picture.

Then Mrs. Rogers saw the furniture.
"The furniture!" she cried.

"Did I dust it well enough?"

asked Amelia Bedelia.

"That's such nice dusting powder."

Mr. Rogers went to wash his hands.

"I say," he called.

"These are very unusual towels."

Mrs. Rogers dashed into the bathroom.

"Oh, my best towels," she said.

"Didn't I change them enough?"
asked Amelia Bedelia.

Mrs. Rogers went to the kitchen.

"I'll cook the dinner.

Where is the rice

I asked you to measure?"

"I put it back in the container.

But I remember—

it measured four and a half inches,"

said Amelia Bedelia.

"Was the meat delivered?"

asked Mrs. Rogers.

"Yes," said Amelia Bedelia.

"I trimmed the fat just like you said.

It does look nice."

Mrs. Rogers rushed to the icebox.

She opened it.

"Lace! Ribbons!

Oh, dear!" said Mrs. Rogers.

"The chicken—you dressed
the chicken?"
asked Mrs. Rogers.
"Yes, and I found the nicest box
to put him in,"
said Amelia Bedelia.
"Box!" exclaimed Mrs. Rogers.
Mrs. Rogers hurried over to the box.
She lifted the lid.
There lay the chicken.
And he was just as dressed
as he could be.

Mrs. Rogers was angry.

She was very angry.

She opened her mouth.

Mrs. Rogers meant

to tell Amelia Bedelia

she was fired.

But before she could

get the words out,

Mr. Rogers put something

in her mouth.

It was so good

Mrs. Rogers forgot about being angry.

"Lemon-meringue pie!"

she exclaimed.

"I made it to surprise you,"

said Amelia Bedelia happily.

So right then and there

Mr. and Mrs. Rogers decided

that Amelia Bedelia must stay.

And so she did.

Mrs. Rogers learned to say

undust the furniture,

unlight the lights,

close the drapes,

and things like that.

Mr. Rogers didn't care

if Amelia Bedelia

trimmed all

of his steaks with lace.

All he cared about
was having her there
to make lemon-meringue pie.